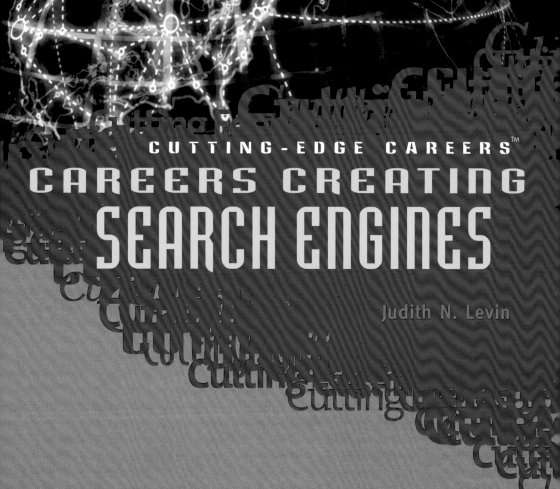

CUTTING-EDGE CAREERS™

CAREERS CREATING
SEARCH ENGINES

Judith N. Levin

ROSEN
PUBLISHING®

New York

For Joann, with thanks

Published in 2007 by The Rosen Publishing Group, Inc.
29 East 21st Street, New York, NY 10010

First Edition

Library of Congress Cataloging-in-Publication Data

Levin, Judith (Judith N.), 1956–
Careers creating search engines / Judith Levin.
    p. cm. — (Cutting-edge careers)
Includes bibliographical references and index.
ISBN-13: 978-1-4042-0957-2
ISBN-10: 1-4042-0957-3 (library binding)
1. Web search engines—Juvenile literature. 2. Search engines—Programming—Juvenile literature. 3. Computer programming—Vocational guidance—Juvenile literature. I. Title.
TK5105.884.L46 2006
025.04—dc22

                                                    2006024486

Manufactured in the United States of America

On the cover: More than 5,500 young people surf the Internet during this campus meeting in Valencia, Spain.

CONTENTS

I N T R O D U C T I O N

ust a few years ago, a career as a Webmaster sounded more like a role in a fantasy game than an actual job. Today, Webmasters—the people who create and maintain Web sites—make up a sizable percentage of the information technology (IT) field. Careers that involve creating, improving, and maintaining Internet search engines are similar to the Webmaster jobs of years past. While few people had heard of these positions in the 1990s, by 2000, there was an unending demand for people who could design and update Web pages.

A search engine is a network of thousands of computers that use indexes to gather and sort relevant information according to a user's requests. Today, the most popular search engine is Google, but there are countless others that appeal to specific audiences. Many of these audiences include scholars or physicians who employ a variety of engines to search for relevant information.

According to the U.S. Department of Labor, high-tech professions in IT will continue growing at a dramatic pace over the next decade. Computer specialists, such as people involved in creating and supporting search engines, are expected to increase by more than two-thirds (more than two million jobs) during that time. The Internet, the World

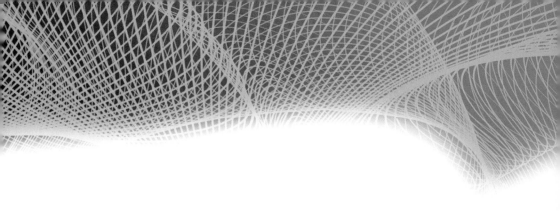

Wide Web, and the technology we use to access them, have so quickly evolved that it's easy to forget that they are new applications. Until a few years ago, they sounded more like science fiction than a marriage of hardware and software. Now, "to Google" is a verb phrase in English, Japanese, German, and Italian.

Search engines, however, are still in their infancy. Most experts guess that we are only seeing 5 percent of what's possible. It's an estimate that surfaces repeatedly. The Internet is still considered one of the world's "wide open spaces." In fact, the Internet and the World Wide Web have attracted Wild West metaphors since the mid-1990s because they are so big that they seem limitless. Like the Wild West, there are few, if any, rules about organizing the information, and the "good" guys and the "bad" guys are perpetually fighting it out. The language of the Web, and of the search engines that we use to find things on it, reflect this analogy. It's part computer-lab talk—which sounds either like math or like people who have stayed up too late working—with such things as algorithms and computer languages that take their names from coffee (Java) or sweet snacks (Gnutella, from Nutella). The other part remains wild: In 2006, Google was advertising for a search engine optimizer with a "white hat hacker mentality" (to fight off the guys with the black hats, of course).

The U.S. Department of Labor's 2006 report on careers estimates that more than 21 million people are working in the computer industry, roughly 16 percent of the national workforce, excluding farming and farm-related jobs. These figures are expected to increase as more and more communication, commerce, educational instruction, and recreation take place online and on an ever-growing number of portable electronic devices.

CHAPTER 1

The Birth
of the Internet

Before there were Internet search engines, there had to be an Internet to search. The first way to link computers was to run physical cables between them. The Internet, literally a network of networks, began in the 1960s with the Advanced Research Projects Agency Network (ARPANET). This U.S. Department of Defense linkage of computers used packet switching (as opposed to circuit switching) to share information. The ability to network computers at that time was largely a way to share expensive technology. But it was also, as the Defense Department discovered, inefficient to continue translating information into different computer languages or to leap from terminal to terminal because the different computers couldn't "talk" to each other.

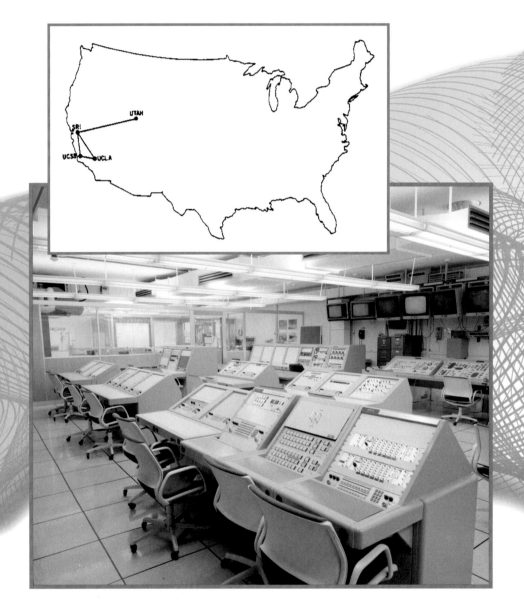

Computers connected to an ARPANET station *(bottom)* transmitted electronic information "packets" to other computers at four universities in the western United States *(top)*.

Once ARPANET was established, computers could easily communicate, even if they ran on different systems and languages, by breaking the message into packets and "shipping" them via a protocol: IP (Internet protocol) and TCP (transmission-control protocol). The packets are then sent out over phone or cable lines or via satellite, and the computer receiving them is able to reconstruct the message.

But ARPANET, later known as the Internet, wasn't a searchable database until the invention of the World Wide Web by Tim Berners-Lee in the late 1980s, a service that became available to the public in 1991. These earliest search tools were not designed to search the World Wide Web because the World Wide Web did not yet exist.

Tim Berners-Lee, the son of two English mathematicians from Manchester University who together built one of England's earliest computers, became a computer programmer himself and invented the World Wide Web in 1991. Berners-Lee created a computer program using hypertext (the links that we use today to automatically cross-reference other documents) to make sharing information easier. His prototype, which he designed with Robert Cailliau, was called ENQUIRE. He continued working on the idea of connected information for years, looking for ways to join ideas together by "hyperlinks."

The World Wide Web

By 1991, Berners-Lee had figured out how to apply his hyperlinks to the Internet, and the World Wide Web was born. Hypertext was conceived and named in 1965 by Ted Nelson, and it is the basis of the World Wide Web—and what makes search engines possible. Nelson imagined computer text that would be nonlinear, so instead of reading a text from beginning to end, one could (in his example) see that someone has quoted something and then go directly to the source of the quotation. We now depend on hyperlinks to give us the ability to maneuver around the World Wide Web.

The British inventor of the World Wide Web, Tim Berners-Lee *(right)* receives Finland's Millennium Technology Prize in 2004 from Finnish president Tarja Halonen for enhancing people's "quality of life."

Web Browsers

But hyperlinked text without any graphics did not attract scores of people to the Internet. It wasn't until the early 1990s when Web browsers were invented that the Internet and World Wide Web exploded in popularity. A Web browser is an application program that allows users to interact with the Internet. Now, instead of dull pages of hyperlinked text, users could enjoy graphics and multimedia applications. The first Web browser, Mosaic, was developed in 1992 by Marc Andreessen and Eric Bina at the National Center for Supercomputing Applications (NCSA). By 1993, Mosaic was available to the public in

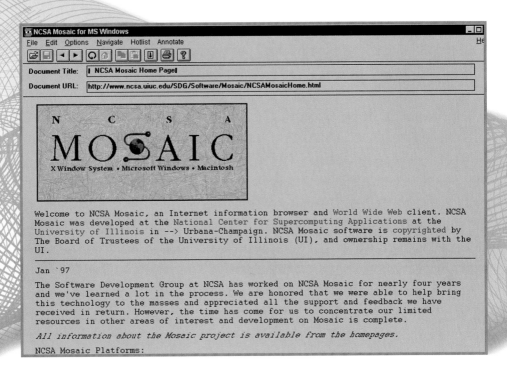

Software engineers at the National Center for Supercomputing Applications (NCSA) designed the Mosaic browser in the early 1990s, followed later by the invention of Netscape Navigator.

versions for Apple Macintosh and Microsoft Windows. Andreessen eventually founded his own company, Netscape Communications Corporation. He, along with his staff, invented the Web browser known to us today as Netscape Navigator.

Early Search Engines and Directories

Alan Emtage, Peter J. Deutsch, and Bill Heelan, students at McGill University in Montreal, Canada, created the first search engine in 1990. They called the tool Archie, short for archive. The program searched file names (not individual pages) of the files located on public anonymous FTP (file transfer protocol) sites and generated a listing of files for a growing database that acted like an index of the content.

A year later, in 1991, Mark McCahill at the University of Minnesota created a computer program called Gopher. Gopher was named for the school's mascot and also for its function: to retrieve information. Gopher indexed plain text documents, as opposed to only file names. In a playful association with the name Archie, the search devices that were used to find documents within the Gopher files were named Veronica and Jughead. (VERONICA also stood for Very Easy Rodent-Oriented Net-wide Index to Computerized Archives.) Veronica allowed users to search by keyword the names of Gopher menu titles.

After the World Wide Web took off, Web sites began to multiply by the thousands and the tens of thousands and the hundreds of thousands. Today, the world's most popular search engine, Google, claims to index more than 4.5 billion distinct Web sites. The question then becomes, how on earth do you find what you're looking for? You can type in the exact Web address (and people do), but that's very limited. The next phase of technology development involved more specific methods to dissect this bounty of information in order to best deliver it to users.

CHAPTER 2

The Evolution of Search Engine Technology

Two approaches to searching the Web developed in the mid-1990s, and both continue to coexist. The first is the directory, sometimes called an Internet index. Human indexers who arrange Web addresses or URLs (uniform resource locators) compile directories by subject. The great advantage, however, is that a genuine human being—generally someone who knows about the subject he or she is compiling sites for—is actually reading and evaluating individual documents. A person, unlike a computer, can scrutinize a document before placing it in an appropriate category. He or she can consider its content and ask, What is this? What does it mean? Is it a site that is worthwhile? In fact, some of today's most popular guides to the Web, such as Yahoo!, began first as directories. Yahoo! was

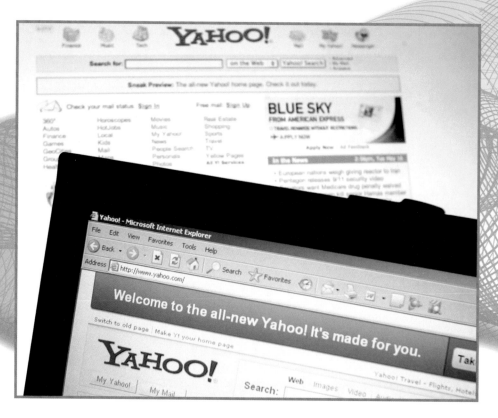

The new Yahoo! Web site, launched in 2006, is seen here on a laptop in front of its earlier version. Web companies continually revise their services to remain competitive.

first called Jerry and David's Guide to the World Wide Web. It was compiled by Jerry Yang and David Filo and published on the Web in 1994 when both of them were working on doctorates at Stanford University. (They had to create their own crawler, a program to seek indexes of information on the Web, because there were no browsers. Mosaic, the first browser, didn't appear until they had been working on the collection for several years.) By 1994, Yahoo! had 100,000 unique visitors. It had become the Internet's first major directory.

The biggest problem of an index—any index—is that it cannot be kept up to date because the Web grows faster than anyone can index it and Web sites change too rapidly. Nevertheless, Web directories remain popular. At least 350 million people continue to rely upon Yahoo! as a Web directory and now use it as a portal to the Internet.

How a Search Engine Works

A search engine takes advantage of the hyperlinks that connect Web sites on the Internet. A software program called a Web crawler automatically browses the Web in a methodical way and sends out inquiries that "crawl" from site to site. Web crawlers are also called Web spiders or Web bots (from "robots"). Web crawlers are not objects that physically move, but rather programs that compile information in specific ways. Web crawlers send out requests to Web addresses on other computers. And it is not one crawler, but 10,000.

Since the crawler is a software program, it is given different instructions on different computers. For instance, WebCrawler, a program launched in 1994, was the first software to index entire Web sites rather than just page titles. Search engine crawlers operate within different sets of instructions or parameters, such as to search titles and first paragraphs only, or to search entire documents, including the metadata. (Metadata, data about data, includes tags that may not be visible when looking at the page and can include the document's title, keywords, the publisher, and other information.) In an effort to more universally create Web content, the Dublin Core Metadata Initiative (DCMI) in 1995 established standards for the Web in fifteen different categories. These standards would eventually facilitate search engine keyword searches and are today often included as a part of the HTML (hypertext markup language) code that is commonly used to create Web pages.

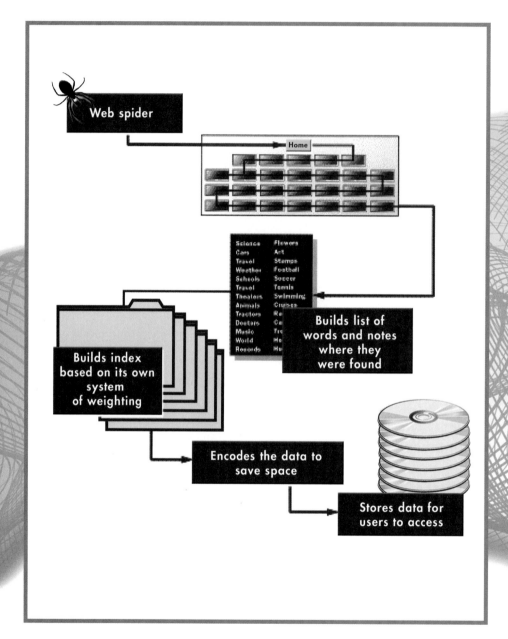

As illustrated here, the flow of information through a search engine follows a set course. A search engine's operating principles may differ depending on the type of search engine used.

The search engine spider goes out checking web pages.

The search finds the home page of each site found.
- ✔ reads the head section of the page
- ✔ reads the page content
- ✔ finds and follows the links

When the spider has finished it's World Wide check of Web pages, it returns home carrying all the details about your Web site.

Data collected by spider

The search engine's database takes the data collected.

List of words found and the page found on

A list of words found and what page they were found on it built.

Index built based on search engines weighting system

The Web pages are indexed based on the search engine's system of indexing.

Data is encoded to save space

The index data is encoded to save on storage space.

Index data stored

The index data is stored and waits for search engine users to perform a search.

Someone visits the search engine and types in a search word or phrase.

Search engine results displayed

The search engine searches it's data and displays the results.

All search engines share fundamental operating principles, as outlined in this illustration. What separated Google from its competitors was the criteria for searching incorporated into its algorithm.

The information the crawler software collects is automatically put into an index. When a query is submitted to a search engine, the query is submitted to that search engine's index. Each search engine has its own index. Thus the index searched by Google is not the same as the one searched by Yahoo! or MSN (Microsoft Network), though some companies have shared indexes. Different search engines vary in the quantity of information they return and what type of information they index. One of the challenges they face is the sifting of data because Web sites are sorted by machines that cannot read or interpret data like humans can. Computers cannot evaluate data like human indexers, who understand exactly what something means or can determine its relevance.

Filtering Unwanted Data

The indexing process must also filter out duplicate information and, of course, spam, the term used to describe not only the unwanted junk mail that comes into your e-mail box but sites created or programmed with manipulated text in order to fool people into visiting them. Spammers who wanted to promote advertising or pornography on the Internet learned simple tricks such as including hidden text on their Web sites to increase visits, or hits. The text was invisible either because it was contained within the programming or because words or phrases were written over and over again in letters that were the same color as the screen.

In the early years of the Internet, search engines were not always equipped to block these manipulated sites. Hence, the Web pages that were returned when people searched "cars" were often pornographic or advertising Web sites that had the word "car" written over and over again in letters not visible to the human eye. The gap between what a software program recognizes and understands and what the human being sees and understands is vast. As it was in the early days and continues to be, the tension between people who create Web sites and the people who create search engines remains considerable.

Keywords

Today's search engines request that the user enter keywords or phrases in a text box on the URL page of the search engine. The place where we come together with the engine on the screen is called the interface. There may be other elements on display, such as advertising banners, but any information contained there is second to search engine functionality. When Google was first being tested for public use, the "human-computer interaction expert" watched everyone load the home page and then just sit there. They explained that they were waiting for the pop-up ads to load, and the weather reports, and the horoscopes. Google's founders originally rejected advertising; they also began only as a search engine. The more visually cluttered sites were "portals"—entrances into many Web destinations often designated by the individual user from various choices offered by the company that was also providing the search engine.

At the time of this writing, Google is also establishing itself as a portal in order to remain competitive. This feature allows Google's individual users to arrange a customized Google Web page that showcases their interests. Still other choices have to do with the question and problems of how humans conduct Web searches. The choices have involved keywords and various ways of combining keywords so that there is at least some chance of finding exactly what you're looking for.

Early Progress, Early Problems

According to Rajeev Motwani, professor of computer science and adviser to Google's cofounder Sergey Brin, searching the Internet in

The U.S. government Web site acts as an Internet portal and offers a different experience for citizens, businesses, or employees. Information about "Jobs" and "Voting" is divided into subheads.

the mid-1990s was dicey, at best. Every year, a new search engine or two debuted: Lycos, WebCrawler, Magellan, Infoseek, Excite, HotBot. But when Motwani tested the new search engine Inktomi by typing in the engine's own name, it couldn't find itself. Simple searches performed in any search engine would typically produce page after page of results in no order whatsoever. The creators of the Yahoo! directory, for instance, spent long hours looking for relevant sites when they were compiling their directory, as did many of the earliest search engine pioneers. At the time, one New York City librarian noted that a search for 1950s beat poets, for one example, produced—in

The Boolean system was named for Irish mathematician, logician, and philosopher George Boole (1815–1864), shown in this illustration from his tenure as professor of mathematics at Queens College in 1860.

no particular order—pages on Allen Ginsberg, gingerbread, and metronomes.

The problems with sorting the information were many. Obtaining poor results was partly a problem of getting people to write their searches more specifically and partly a question of how results were returned. Since search results are often returned in order of relevancy—the number of times your search term appears in a document—being specific about your search could mean the difference between finding what you are searching for or not. And the problems of sorting the information became more and more difficult as the Internet and all of its content grew ever larger.

Yet another way to make your searches more closely match your requests is to use exact phrases in quotations. In this case, the search engine will narrow your query by defining the order of words as you expect them to appear in the returned documents since it knows to discard those results where the words don't appear next to each other in the correct order.

The Boolean System

One way to make Internet searches more effective was to use the Boolean system, named for George Boole, a nineteenth-century mathematician. The Boolean system is based on set theory: if you cross the set containing hot dogs with the set containing mustard with the set containing relish, you get a search that produces a hot dog with mustard and relish. A Boolean query is the kind that invites you to include the commands "and," "or," and "not," and it had already existed as a way of querying a database. The Boolean system is famous for being counter-intuitive: to get your above-mentioned hot dog as you ordered it, you actually have to specify mustard or relish. And, although it can be useful, it does not match the way most people think. But using the "advanced search" option in 2006 for Google, Yahoo!, or many other search engines, one is led into a more natural way of posing a Boolean query. Searchers can specify a whole phrase or phrases that they want to find plus words that must be included (the equivalent of "and") and words that cannot be included (the equivalent of "not").

Natural Language Processing

Some non-Boolean systems attempted to utilize "natural language" processing. AskJeeves, a search engine launched in 1996 and now known simply as Ask, first allowed users to ask questions just as they would if they were in conversation with another person. Instead of "President and U.S. and 1856," someone could ask "Who was President of the U.S. in 1856?" But the results didn't deliver as well as expected. Non-Boolean systems have since improved but are

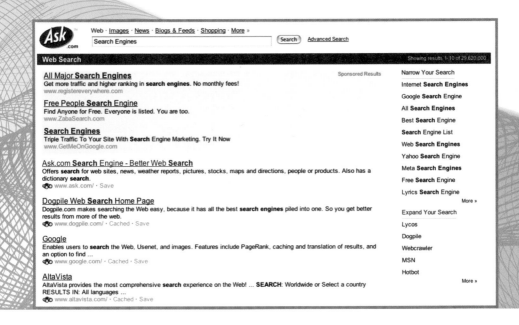

In addition to listing results from a user's query, the search engine Ask.com also lists related topics in the right-hand margin to broaden or narrow a person's choices.

still limited by the inability of computers to process natural language well. Many modern search engines can answer simple queries such as "How do I get from Denver to Salt Lake City?" They have been programmed to recognize "from" [place] "to" [place] as a request for directions.

One of the problems of posing queries in natural language remains that if you tell a computer you're looking for a mustang, for example, it doesn't know if you mean the horse or the car. If you tell it you want information about "a 1990 fire-engine red sports car," it's going to deliver results about "fire engines," not about "a used MG, good condition." Computers match words, but they do not make associations or recognize synonyms. This is a limitation that software writers hope to change.

CHAPTER 3

The Rise of Google

In 1996, Larry Page, Google's cofounder, discovered that using a new search engine called AltaVista produced not just a list of Web sites but a list of highlighted links. Those same hyperlinks had make the World Wide Web into a web that Tim Berners-Lee had decided to highlight and that crawlers now crawl to produce an index. He and Sergey Brin, both Ph.D. students at the University of Stanford's School of Computer Science, decided to use these links as the basis to order search results.

In the academic world, especially in the sciences, the importance of a research article can be established or even quantified by counting the number of times other researchers refer to it in their printed works, or how many times it is cited.

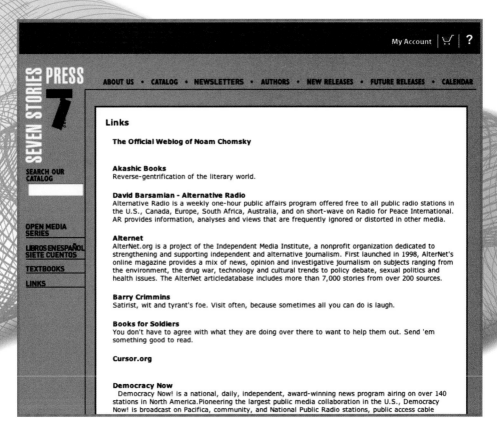

This screen grab from the Seven Stories Press Web site includes hyperlinks that connect readers with authors' names, books they have written, and books with related content.

Hyperlinks, decided Page, could be used like citations. An incoming hyperlink to a Web site was like an endorsement saying that the Web site had merit or was important. He would evaluate the worth of the incoming links on the same basis. If many Web pages were linked to one Web site, then that site would come back early on in the list of results for a query concerning the subjects of that site. It was a way to rank the importance and relevance of individual Web pages to one single query, and Page dubbed the system PageRank, in part a pun on

Google founders Larry Page *(left)* and Sergey Brin pose on Google's campus headquarters in Mountain View, California. They founded the technology company in 1998.

his own name. PageRank would later be the basis of the famous, secret, and often-refined Google algorithm. (An algorithm is a set of mathematical equations.) Other elements of PageRank that influenced search results included how close together keywords appeared and whether they were capitalized or lowercase.

In 1997, Google became the basis of a search engine for use by Stanford students and faculty. It was named "Google" for googolplex (the number one followed by a googol—or 100 zeros), and it captured their sense of the hugeness of the amount of data that existed on the Web. At the time, Google was the only search engine using anything like a page-ranking algorithm that returned results in order of relevance. It quickly became the search engine of choice on the Stanford campus. The domain name was registered on September 15, 1997, and the company was incorporated one year later. Still, it took a while for Google to make a profit. Although Page and Brin originally wanted to sell the patent, they found no immediate buyers and instead went into business for themselves.

In a 2002 television interview with Jim Lehrer, Larry Page described the search engine process: "Your search gets sent out to hundreds or thousands of computers and they all work on it for a short amount of time, a tenth of a second. And then they send back all their information and the computers put it all back together and send it to you [to answer your query]."

Internet Advertising

One of the issues was that no one could figure out how a search engine could made money, especially if, like Google, it refused to allow people to pay for inclusion (or placement) within it. Advertising was clearly one option, though Google wanted to exclude annoying pop-up or banner advertisements in order to maintain its reputation for clean design, user friendliness, and usability. The answer became the selling

Pictured here is an example of spam advertisements that are programmed to automatically open a series of pop-up images whenever you read an advertiser's e-mail.

of text advertisements along the sides of the pages after Google had returned initial lists of search results. Earning a profit through advertising has become crucial for the survival of search engines, especially since the keywords used for a search can automatically determine which advertising a person views on his or her computer. A person's interests can be linked to specific advertisements—not pop-up, blinking, or "singing" banner ads that appear regardless of the search. These ads are tied to the subject that the user is searching, thereby targeting an audience. Search engines differ in whether they mix these results into the "natural" or "organic" results that appear as the answer to the user's query or whether they are discretely listed on the side or top as "sponsored" results, a phrase that turned out to be more profitable than calling them advertisements. The search engine receives a profit when the ad is clicked on, and the company targets people who may actually be looking for them. Some of the companies buy formulas that simply plug the search phrase into a sentence, producing results like "shop for discount cosmetics on eBay!" But as advertising and search technology iron out their formulas, what emerges is a way to advertise that is far more cost effective than television or direct mail advertising because it is targeted to the individual user.

Search Engine Optimization

At this time, new industries that combined search engines and advertising sprung up: search engine marketing and search engine optimization. Both of these jobs are closely tied to the industry. The search engine optimizers (SEOs) market their ability to understand search engine algorithms and "fix" Web sites so that they will appear in the top rankings (the first page or two of a user's search results). Improved Web site rankings obviously mean a greater audience share and the potential to increase profits. Some search engine optimization involves the legitimate tweaking of keywords on the Web page and inserting metatags that will insure that the search engine's crawlers respond.

But the boundary between "optimizing" a page and creating spam has not been very clear. General guidelines claim that it is legitimate to do something to a Web site that helps the page's user and not legitimate to manipulate it in ways that simply bring it traffic. Still, spam manages to influence the search results and, during the periodic adjustments of the algorithm, Web pages get wildly reordered. Legitimate Web sites sometimes get rejected as spam or are sent far down the results list out of the user's immediate view. And the "black hat" (as opposed to "white hat") manipulators of Web sites have learned how easy it is to create dummy sites with dummy links to the page being "optimized."

Bloggers have also learned "Google bombing," creating so many links to a site that it will appear as the first result for a given inquiry. The intent of bloggers is more likely to be humor or a political statement than financial gain, as when they succeeded in making George W. Bush's biography at the official Whitehouse.gov Web site the top ranked result for the search "miserable failure" on three major search engines. The optimizers, spammers, and "bombers" kept the search engines busy adjusting their algorithms as the search engine business became not just big business, but the future of advertising.

New Methods

In April 2006, Google purchased a new search engine algorithm, Orion, from Ori Allon, a twenty-six-year-old Ph.D. candidate at the University of New South Wales, in Australia. They also hired Allon. Historically, Google has not revamped its engine so that it hasn't seemed unfamiliar, but rather it incorporates new features or technologies. The key benefits of Orion seem to be that it can gather results not only by keyword but also by words that are associated to the keyword, a function with which all search engines have struggled. It's not yet clear whether the engine, as improved by Allon, will know that a search for a sports car should send you to an MG, but it will, to use his example, take a query about the American Revolution and return results about American history, as well as George Washington and the Declaration of Independence. Orion's other advantage is that it can display excerpts of the relevant pages without the user having to leave the search engine site.

Another approach search engines are taking is clustering. Mooter and Vivísimo, for example, are two search engines that will take a query about "bass" and immediately break it into clusters of

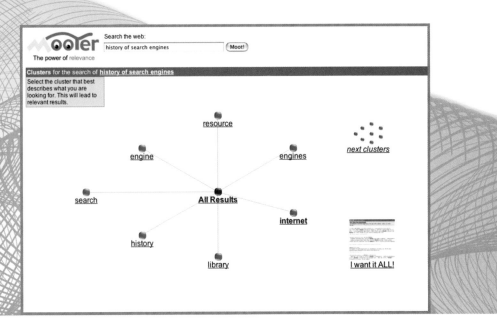

By using the search engine Mooter, users are directed to a set of results configured in a cluster. Clicking on each topic in the cluster will bring users specific results.

related information. What that means is that the results for the fish called bass will be separated from those concerning the musical instrument, the beer brand name, or the shoe manufacturer. Given these options, the person conducting the search can start in the right ballpark, at least, immediately eliminating Web sites that are totally irrelevant. Mooter will also personalize rankings as the user makes choices, using artificial intelligence to interpret feedback from user behavior.

The search engine Teoma (the Gaelic word for "expert") uses authorities on subjects to rank results and identify key authoritative pages. These have been established by looking at subject-specific communities. Paul Gardi, former president and CEO of Teoma, explained in 2004, "When you get down to the local level [which he says Google does not], you will find that links cluster around certain subjects or themes, very much like communities." Future search engines will undoubtedly utilize experts to sort information or they will instead be programmed using artificial intelligence and frequent user preferences.

CHAPTER 4

Jobs Creating
Search Engines

The U.S. Department of Labor's *Occupational Outlook Handbook* publishes America's official breakdown of industries and specific jobs within industries. Each position is profiled detailing the job's specific duties, average working conditions, market conditions, and average salaries. The Department of Labor also publishes the number of workers in each industry and how these numbers are expected to change over a decade. Before examining specific career opportunities that are related to creating search engines, successful job candidates should consider the following traits useful:

Experience with various computer hardware and software systems and processes

A clear understanding of several programming languages such as C++ and Java

Genuine interest in the future of computing capabilities

A methodical, practical, and logical approach to problem-solving techniques

Solid communication and math skills

Excellent sense of creativity and self-discipline

The stamina to work independently

The desire for continuing education as technology evolves

Computer Programmers

The 2006 U.S. Department of Labor bulletin describes computer programmers as people who "write, test, and customize" the detailed software that computers follow. Computer programmers write software programs that tell computers how to access and process data. Programmers use, among others, object-oriented computer languages such as C++ and Java. (Other useful languages include Perl, HTML, Visual Basic, Visual C+++, and CASE tools.) The U.S. Department of Labor notes that computer programmers, like other computer specialists, are largely required to have college degrees. Those seeking jobs as computer programmers should have a bachelor's degree in computer science, mathematics, or information systems, although an associate's degree or technology certificate will be enough for some jobs, depending on the technical skills that are needed. A computer programmer who is hoping to advance to systems analyst

BEYOND GOOGLE

There are plenty of search engine options that will lead to a world of discovery beyond Google. Below is a list of the most popular:

LookSmart.com: LookSmart is a search engine that features categories to narrow your Internet search such as "Health," "Education," "Sports," and "Style." In addition, it features an alphabetical listing of the links of print publications on its home page. Other resources include "Resources" and "Web Picks."

Ask.com: Ask.com has a variety of "human" tools to help people search including a dictionary and encyclopedia, as well as a way to search images, news, and maps. Ask.com also has a link to search popular blogs.

AltaVista.com: AltaVista.com, the Web's first full-text database, divides user categories into groups such as Web pages, MP3 files, images, video, and news. In addition, it allows users to narrow their searching fields by country and/or language. Another bonus is its "Babel Fish" language translator.

Dmoz.com: Dmoz.com is the Web's largest open human-edited directory run entirely by volunteers. Its home page is divided into approximately twenty categories, each one a link to a larger list of more specific categories. For instance, one click on the "Arts" category leads users to a large variety of related categories, each with hundreds (or thousands) of Web pages.

Mooter.com: Mooter.com uses Web clustering to help users narrow their search. For instance, a search of "photography" produces the following options: "art," "history," "nature," "accessories," and "resources," each one its own link to further specify results.

will benefit from business experience such as accounting or a business degree.

The U.S. Department of Labor predicts less growth (8.4 percent for the period between 2004 and 2014) for computer programmers than for some other technology specialists. Its report accounted for 22 percent of the computer specialists in the area of IPs, Web search portals, and data processing services.

Students seeking jobs as computer programmers should take as many math classes as possible, including algebra, geometry, calculus, and even statistics if it is offered. Obviously, most future programmers will attend college, but for those who opt out of a four-year degree, seeking certification as a computer professional could help you learn the skills to get hired. Seek work as a programmer trainee in a large company, apply for internships, take state and federal civil service exams for entry-level programming, or apply for certification in various computer languages until you gain enough experience to enter the job market.

As of May 2004, the median hourly wage of computer programmers was $31.39 (about $65,000 annually); however, in a December 2005 *San Francisco Chronicle* article, Google was identified as the employer that pushed the average salary of computer programmers in the San Francisco area to $85,840 (up from $66,270 in 1999 when Google was first gaining ground). As a result, competing jobs may pay in ranges that are slightly higher, depending on the region where the positions are located. Computer programmers typically work a forty-hour week, though hours can be longer and overtime is sometimes available, depending on the employer. A benefits package is typically included as a part of an applicant's annual salary and may include health care, retirement benefits, paid sick days, vacation days, and holidays. Stock options are sometimes made available, too, depending on the employer.

Students in most computer classes have the opportunity to work on individual laptops while following along with an instructor in a traditional way.

Software Engineers

The largest group of computer specialists being hired at Google are software engineers, often just called computer engineers. Software engineers must be able to understand computer programming and various languages, but they generally focus on software development. These computer specialists design, develop, test, and evaluate software programs before they are made available to the public. In some cases, software engineers must also possess strong computer programming skills, with the languages C, C++, and Java being most important. Software engineers often work in a team environment depending on the client's needs. In 2004, there were about 800,000 software engineers in the United States according to the Department of Labor, but this number is expected to grow more rapidly than other occupations over the next decade.

Many of the most interesting jobs at Google are in software development, and many departments are also now requesting that potential employees understand more about computer-human interaction and user interface design and testing. These applications, and especially software that involves functions that use artificial intelligence, demand that potential applicants have at least some background in human behavioral psychology. Eventually, taking college classes in human psychology will become necessary for everyone seeking positions in software engineering.

While the Department of Labor says computer engineers "usually have at least a bachelor's degree in computer science, software engineering, or computer information systems," it also notes that employers value more advanced degrees. It is also a good idea to have experience working with a wide range of computer languages and operating systems. Software engineers must be able to explain what they want to the computer programmer, so the ability to communicate well across a wide range of technologies is highly valued.

Software engineers Andres Salmon *(left)* and Chuck Black process compact discs to stream online at Musicmatch, a digital music jukebox service in Rancho Bernardo, California.

Most of the innovation taking place with specific search engine companies such as Google and Yahoo! is also occurring in software design, so the number of software engineers needed between 2004 and 2014 is expected to skyrocket by more than 56 percent. The U.S. Department of Labor reports $36.16 per hour as the median salary of computer software engineers, or about $75,000 annually. The more experience a person has in his or her field obviously

Phillip Olexa, a high school senior from Columbia, South Carolina, looks for computer-related career opportunities at the 2006 Clemson University Career Fair in Clemson, South Carolina.

increases his or her earning potential. The highest paid software engineers can earn upward of $115,000 annually, with the majority of positions offering substantial benefits packages, including paid sick and vacation time, health care, retirement savings accounts, and stock options. Software engineers typically work a forty-hour week.

Highly skilled and experienced software engineers have the potential to become consultants, often a choice that offers a higher salary and the ability to work fewer hours. Consultants are often hired as freelance employees for temporary jobs. In 2004, there were approximately 23,000 freelance software engineers employed at various firms throughout the United States.

Students who desire a future working as software engineers should, like other computer enthusiasts, take as many classes in mathematics as possible. Gaining a familiarity with various operating systems, computer languages, and writing basic programs will also be useful. Most college students interested in software engineering major in computer science or computer information systems. College students may also benefit from summer internship programs, as

well as co-op education programs offered through specific schools. When searching for that first job, potential software engineers should consider large companies with extensive training programs, mentoring opportunities, and a steady growth rate. Be prepared to continue your education as needed to keep abreast of key develop-ments in technology. Traveling has also recently been a factor in some companies, as more and more firms are outsourcing jobs to foreign countries.

Computer Systems Analysts

Computer systems analyst positions that are related to creating search engines largely handle data storage and provide technical support to large computer networks. According to a 2005 California Projections of Employment report, job growth for systems analysts is expected to skyrocket by at least 52 percent over the next decade. There were nearly 50,000 systems analysts working at various firms in California alone during 2005.

Computer systems analysts are generally creative problem-solvers. They are able to dissect entire networks of computers and determine how to best maintain them, update their capabilities, increase their storage capacities, and improve their overall efficiency. To this end, the most sought-after systems analysts possess a combination of intellectual, technical, and interpersonal skills. They must also be excellent communicators to explain the projected needs of a search engine or a company's network of computers and data storage systems as they (or the Web itself) expand.

The median annual salary for systems analysts in 2004 was approximately $92,570, according to the U.S. Department of Labor, but salaries could top out at more than $107,000 per year depending on a person's level of experience and technical expertise. All employers are seeking only those individuals who have at least earned a four-year degree, and some require graduate degrees as well. Once employed, top earners also scored better-than-average benefits packages. Some packages can include such perks as expense accounts, stock options, and frequent financial incentives such as deadline-oriented and end-of-the-year bonuses.

Students who are interested in pursuing careers as computer systems analysts should also take as many math and computer classes as possible, both in high school and college. Again, the most highly sought after applicants will be extremely versatile in various computer languages and operating systems. Among the ways in which prospective systems analysts can gain experience and exposure to different computer networks is by seeking internships and company training and mentoring programs.

CHAPTER 5

Search Engines of the Future

One major obstacle that remains in place when writing about the future of the Internet is that it is a technology that is always changing. A librarian at the New York Public Library of Science and Business said, "You can't write about the future of search engines; anything you'd write has either happened this morning and we don't know it yet, or else it's [a technology that hasn't appeared] yet." What do people want from search engines? How will information be classified in the future? The librarian was right; our methods of searching information are changing as rapidly as the Internet itself.

Many people put the goals of search engines into exactly the same terms: They say they want computers to use natural language so that they can ask questions and have computers

Jon S. von Tetzchner, CEO of Opera Software, demonstrates how new Web browsers work on portable digital gadgets such as the BlackBerry.

answer them as a human would. (From a technological standpoint, that's employing what is known as artificial intelligence—having a computer estimate a response based on a set of controlled factors, better voice recognition, and natural language inquiry.)

The future of search engine technology isn't going in just one direction except insofar as it is all moving toward creating a world in which every device (laptops, PDAs, cell phones) is searchable. This desire of mobilizing constant "live" search abilities across platforms requires compatibility between operating systems and languages.

Vertical Search Engines

Another method in which engineers and designers are controlling the ever-expanding Web is by making it smaller, or at least narrower, in various ways. Vertical search engines work to decrease the expansiveness of the Web by making the search subject more specific. If you want to go shopping, for instance, specific search engines narrow the field by filtering out irrelevant results. Another vertical search engine, GlobalSpec, will go deep into the Web and produce results not otherwise available. Not only does GlobalSpec use human editors to identify about 100,000 sites, but it crawls parts of the "invisible Web," which is one of the targets of many search-of-the-future projects. GlobalSpec includes databases that are not accessible via standard search engines because they include subscriber-based materials that are not available to the general public.

John Battelle, cofounding editor of *Wired* magazine, founder of *The Industry Standard*, and author of *Search*, calls GlobalSpec a "domain specific search engine" and notes that because it deals with a narrow field and a smaller domain, it is able to get better results with simpler queries. Additionally, it is able to return results on subjects related to the query. Battelle suggests that one future for search engine applications is a world in which more subjects will become the subject of vertical searches, and then a major search engine provider such as Google will become the metasearch engine that will crawl those vertical search results.

Other Search Methods

Search results may also be narrowed through the use of tagging and file-sharing software. In these cases, visitors to a site mark it or comment on it. This community of like-minded people thereby produces a set of results narrowed by their common interests. This process of tagging Web sites is called folksonomy—"folks" plus "taxonomy."

Local searches, or Web searches that are confined to results that have a physical location in common, are predicted to become much

An employee of Japanese mobile communications company KDDI displays a new mobile handset by Toshiba that has a camera, stereo speakers, and GPS navigation in 3-D.

more important in the coming years. Local searches involve the ability to inform your computer, cell phone, or PDA that you're in ZIP code 11743. Suppose you want a pizza but you don't know where to place an order? Instantly, you have all the data that you need to order a pie from any of the restaurants within your ZIP code. This is present, not future, technology and, increasingly, at least some of the computers already know where they are through personalized settings. A cell phone or PDA linked to the Global Positioning System (GPS) knows where you are by satellite.

One of the limitations of a conventional search is that it is heavily dependent on HTML—the hypertext markup language that makes links work. But HTML is based on words, and that makes search engines clumsy when it comes to retrieving pictures or videos or music. Of course, if they are tagged, the crawlers can index them. Flickr, a Web site that indexes hundreds of thousands of photos, has access to sort those images, but the tags are verbal.

Recent research into search engine technology involves visual searches. Scirus, a search engine for scientific information, allows users to draw an image—even a 3-D image—with a mouse and then search for similar results in its database but not yet within the Web. After all, engineers and designers may be searching for a shape, not a verbal description, and "sort of looks like a hammer, but pointy" is not going to return images of a hatchet. Search engines that utilize visual imagery remain limited, but the technology is already here and it may be available on a wider basis in the future. Search engine creators imagine that users will one day be able to search for an exact visual image that they remember from a movie or a photograph. Other similar technology will allow users to play a few bars of a song or a piece of music on a virtual keyboard in order to access a complete recording of the entire song.

One of the fantasies in the world of search is that of mobile visual search technology. John Battelle imagines pointing your cell phone at

Toshiba scientist Takahiro Kawamura explains a new software program that allows its users to take a snapshot of a product's bar code to glean further information about it on the Internet.

the bar code of a product in a store and receiving information about it—everything from user reviews to whether the product was made using child labor—including where in the neighborhood you might buy it less expensively. This fantasy requires your cell phone to read bar codes. It also requires all merchants to make the databases of their inventories searchable. It remains future technology, but technology that will likely be achievable within the next decade.

But another Battelle prediction that is coming true is the use of Mobot, a visual search technology that utilizes a camera phone and any wireless carrier. Instead of typing on a keypad, the user takes a picture of an ad, a product catalog, or a magazine and immediately connects to information about it, without URLs or bar codes. Battelle imagines, however, that we will one day have the technology to point a camera phone at anything and receive information about it—in a museum for instance.

User Preferences and Artificial Intelligence

One of the most exciting developments in search engine technology is the use of user preferences to narrow the search field. In part, this technology already exists: A personalized Google toolbar, for example, is a data collection device, and the "clustering" search engines such as Mooter refine a user's search by gradually honing in on the user's desires. The most useful image of this kind of search, however, may be the way the Amazon database functions. Amazon uses artificial intelligence to greet you by name. The database remembers past purchases, as well as what items you have viewed recently, and it offers customized recommendations based on past choices. Finally, Amazon produces a customized home page listing your favorite categories and offers you related media suggestions such as CDs by an artist to whom you have listened in the past or the latest book by your favorite author. Amazon also recommends products that have been bought by people who have bought the same things you have. Additionally, it posts reviews of products, both from experts and from other customers, and invites responses to both. Amazon contains your entire search history and uses that history—either to help you or attempt to sell you things—depending on your viewpoint. Years ago, Amazon was only a database, but it is now linked to the A9 search engine, which uses clustering and remembers your search history.

Google's motto is "organizing the world's information and making it accessible." To that end, the company has gradually added a variety of specific functions to its search engine applications, including Froogle, a local shopping search engine; Google Maps, which provides

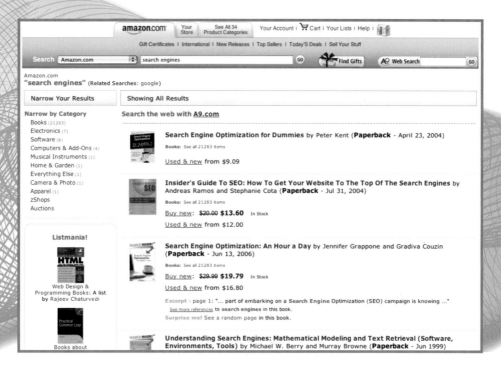

The popular Web site Amazon.com uses data mined from previous visits to make suggestions to returning consumers as a way to appeal to them as individuals and increase sales.

maps and directions; Google News, a news service that users can customize; and g-mail, Google's e-mail service.

What else does the future of search engines hold? Imagine "searching" for your lost luggage from your PDA or cell phone, which a search engine will be able to find because your suitcase will be tagged with a microchip. Imagine a world in which everything is wired and everything is linked. We will go from using our phone to look up television sitcoms to being able to reset the air conditioner in our homes before arriving home, and checking in with our parents or siblings on our video wristwatch.

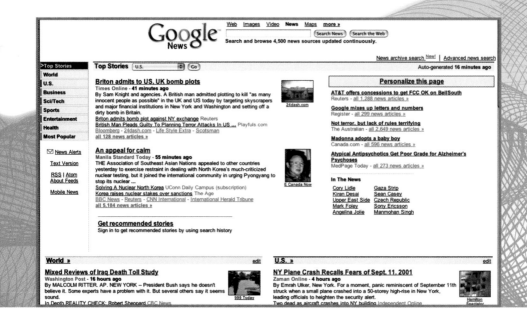

Google is continually expanding services. This screen grab of the Web site features international news and offers users the ability to personalize the page according to their interests.

Potentially everything in your clickstream—every Web site you've ever clicked on—and the music you've downloaded, the videos and television programs that you've watched, every e-mail you've ever sent or received, and the hard drive of your computer and everything stored on it could be combined into a single database. Put it together and you get, potentially, either a search engine that would be very helpful in guessing what you want or a serious invasion of your privacy. It depends on who has access to the information and what uses will be applied to the data.

It's not as if someone is reading our e-mail and Web searches in real time, but it is being crawled for keywords that advertisers have bought. When Google launched g-mail, for instance, having failed to

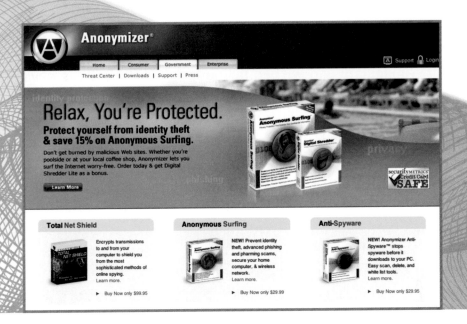

The Web site Anonymizer.com offers software that provides users with anonymous searches, defending users from privacy and security threats on the Internet.

warn people that small advertisements would appear next to their mail based on its content, users were extremely displeased.

From a research point of view, this sort of keyword identification system merely raises questions about what happens when you become interested in new things. In some cases, users may be able to request that the computer simply ignore past preferences. From the standpoint of privacy, it results in legal issues, which will no doubt employ lawyers, if not computer engineers, and the need for more software that allows people to browse the Internet anonymously, using, for instance, anonymizer.com. It might also make us hope that the Web sites that collect information about us are very, very secure.

The Intelligent Web

Yet for the imaginary and wished-for perfect search, Battelle says that even tags and clickstreams and the computer learning your preferences won't be enough. He says we need an "intelligent" or "semantic Web," which is what World Wide Web creator Tim Berners-Lee called it. The intelligent/semantic Web would be able to use reason or, more precisely, logic. Battelle gives a simple example of what that means from a 2002 essay by Paul Ford. If Jim has a friend named Paul, then Paul has a friend named Jim. The intelligent Web would be able to find the statement "Jim is a friend of Paul's" and then, if you did a search for "Paul's friends," the search engine would be able to return Jim's name, even if it didn't appear in Paul's Web site. The search engine would have made a logical leap.

The semantic/intelligent Web is the model for IBM's WebFountain. It is, as Battelle describes it, a platform used by corporate clients that allows for very specific and detailed queries (and requires the knowledge of how to ask them). It can, for instance, answer a query such as, "Give me all the documents on the Web that have at least one page of content in Arabic, are located in the Midwest, and are connected to at least two similar documents but are not connected to the official Al Jazeera Web site, and mention anyone on a specific list of terrorist suspects." WebFountain accomplishes this by crawling and indexing the Web (like any search engine does, but it can crawl the entire Web in one day instead of in a month) and then classifies and retags the entire Web as needed by a specific customer, using semantic categories.

For the present, it looks as though the future of search engines is everywhere—in all languages, on all media. The job listings that the big engine/portals like Yahoo! and Google post show you a bit about where search is going. They have posted jobs for people to develop 3-D software, to design better interfaces for mobile devices, to work with video and film technology, and to identify marketing trends that shape user behavior when watching television. These include, but are not limited to, the intersection of Internet and television technologies, video-on-demand services, personal video recorders, and the emergence of next generation set-top boxes with IP connectivity.

GLOSSARY

algorithm A set of mathematical equations.

ARPANET (Advanced Research Projects Agency Network) A network of computers developed by the U.S. Department of Defense that was the precursor to today's Internet.

artificial intelligence (AI) A specific branch of computer science that studies and creates ways in which computers will act more like humans or mimic human behavior.

clickstream The virtual "trail" that a user leaves when surfing the Internet.

database A collection of organized electronic documents that are generally searchable by one or more means.

googolplex The number one followed by a googol, or 100 zeros.

hyperlink An element in an electronic document that users can click on to link that document to a totally different document.

index A list of keywords that are used in database design to make it faster to find and sort specific information.

interface Place where two different things meet and communicate with each other. A user interface, or customer interface, allows a user to communicate with a computer's operating system.

metadata Information about data that describes how, when, and by whom the information was collected. Metadata is essential for XML-based Web applications.

packet A bit of information transported over a packet-switching network.

portal A Web site that offers a broad array of resources and services, such as e-mail, forums, and search engines.

protocol An agreed-upon formula for sharing information between two devices.

prototype An original form or model on which later models are based.

query A request that is sent through a search engine, usually with keywords.

search engine A network of thousands of computers that use indexes to gather and sort relevant information according to a user's requests.

semantic Web An extension of the current World Wide Web that allows information to be reclassified and shared more easily.

spam Electronic "junk" mail; unwanted or unsolicited e-mail.

tag A command inserted within a document such as a Web page that specifies how it should be formatted.

taxonomy A specific arrangement or order; a way to classify information.

Web browser A software application used to locate and display Web pages.

Web spider A software application that fetches Web pages and feeds them to search engines; Web spiders are also known as Web bots.

World Wide Web (WWW) A system of Internet servers using a language or formatting that allows users to link from one document or file to another by clicking hyperlinks.

FOR MORE INFORMATION

Computer History Museum
1401 N. Shoreline Boulevard
Mountain View, CA 94043
(650) 810-1010
Web site: http://www.computerhistory.org

Google Headquarters
1600 Amphitheatre Parkway
Mountain View, CA 94043
Web site: http://www.google.com/jobs/students.html

Institute for the Certification of Computer Professionals (ICCP)
2350 East Devon Avenue, Suite 115
Des Plaines, IL 60018-4610
(800) 843-8227
Web site: http://www.iccp.org

International Webmasters Association
119 East Union Street, Suite F
Pasadena, CA 91103
(626) 449-3709
Web site: http://www.iwanet.org

National Workforce Center for Emerging Technologies
3000 Landerholm Circle S.E. N258

Bellevue, WA 98007-6484
(425) 564-4215
Web site: http://www.nwcet.org

Netscape World Headquarters
P.O. Box 7050
Mountain View, CA 94039-7050
(650) 254-1900
Web site: http://channels.netscape.com/ns/info/default.jsp

Society for Industrial and Applied Mathematics (SIAM)
3600 University City Science Center
Philadelphia, PA 19104-2688
(800) 447-7426
Web site: http://www.siam.org

Web Sites

Due to the changing nature of Internet links, Rosen Publishing has developed an online list of Web sites related to the subject of this book. This site is updated regularly. Please use this link to access the list:

http://www.rosenlinks.com/cec/sear

FOR FURTHER READING

Battelle, John. *The Search: How Google and Its Rivals Rewrote the Rules of Business and Transformed Our Culture*. New York, NY: Portfolio Hardcover, 2005.

Berners-Lee, Tim. *Weaving the Web: The Original Design and Ultimate Destiny of the World Wide Web*. New York, NY: HarperCollins, 1999.

Graham, Ian. *Internet Revolution*. Chicago, IL: Heinemann Library, 2003.

Hafner, Katie, and Matthew Lyon. *Where Wizards Stay Up Late: The Origins of the Internet*. New York, NY: Simon & Schuster, 1996.

Hertzfeld, Andy. *Revolution in the Valley*. Sebastapol, CA: O'Reilly, 2004.

Kaplan, David. *The Silicon Boys and Their Valley of Dreams*. New York, NY: Harper, 2000.

Laing, Gordon. *Digital Retro: The Evolution and Design of the Personal Computer*. San Francisco, CA: Sybex, 2005.

Langville, Amy N. *Google's PageRank and Beyond: The Science of Search Engine Rankings*. Princeton, NJ: Princeton University Press, 2006.

Lewis, Michael. *Next: The Future Just Happened*. New York, NY: Norton, 2001.

Markoff, John. *What the Dormouse Said: How the 60s Counterculture Shaped the Personal Computer*. New York, NY: Viking, 2005.

Tracy, Kathleen. *Marc Andreessen and the Development of the Web Browser*. Bear, DE: Mitchell Lane Publishers, 2002.

Vise, David A. *The Google Story*. New York, NY: Delacorte Press, 2005.

BIBLIOGRAPHY

Battelle, John. *The Search: How Google and Its Rivals Rewrote the Rules of Business and Transformed Our Culture.* New York, NY: Portfolio Hardcover, 2005.

"The Complete Guide to Googlemania." *Wired*, March 2004. Retrieved June 24, 2006 (http://www.wired.com/wired/ archive/12.03/google.html).

Fielden, Ned L., and Lucy Kuntz. *Search Engines Handbook.* Jefferson, NC: McFarland & Co., 2002.

Graham, Jefferson. "The Search Engine That Could." *USA Today*, August 23, 2003. Retrieved June 24, 2006 (http://www. usatoday.com/tech/news/2003-08-25-google_x.htm).

Hammonds, Keith. "How Google Grows . . . and Grows . . . and Grows." *Fast Company*, April 2003. Retrieved June 23, 2006 (http://www.fastcompany.com/magazine/69/google.html).

Reid, Robert H. *Architects of the Web: 1,000 Days that Built the Future of Business.* New York, NY: John Wiley & Sons, Inc., 1997.

Sherman, Chris. "The Technology Behind Google." *Search Engine Watch*, August 12, 2002. Retrieved June 23, 2006. (http://www. searchenginewatch.com/searchday/02/sd0812-googletech.html).

Tracy, Kathleen. *Marc Andreessen and the Development of the Web Browser.* Bear, DE: Mitchell Lane Publishers, 2002.

INDEX

About the Author

Judith N. Levin is an author and librarian with a variety of nonfiction books to her credit, most of which were written for young adults on a variety of subjects including history, science, and technology. Although she made it through college with a manual typewriter, she now could not live without her computer and the Internet.

Photo Credits

Cover (top) © www.istockphoto.com/Perry Kroll; cover (bottom) © Jose Jordan/AFP/Getty Images; pp. 4–5 Bruce Rolff/Shutterstock.com; p. 8 (bottom) Library of Congress Prints and Photographs Division, HAER CAL, 42-LOMP, 1A-56; p. 10 © Martti Kainulainen/AFP/Getty Images; p. 11 courtesy of the National Center for Supercomputing Applications (NCSA) and the board of trustees of the University of Illinois; p. 14 © Justin Sullivan/Getty Images; p. 20 www.firstgov.gov; p. 21 © Keystone/Hulton Archive/Getty Images; p. 23 www.ask.com; p. 25 www.sevenstories.com/links; p. 26 © Kim Kulish/Corbis; p. 31 www.mooter.com/moot; p. 37 Lee Morris/Shutterstock.com; p. 39 © Sandy Huffaker/AP/Wide World Photos; pp. 40–41 © Ken Ruinard/Anderson Independent-Mail/AP/Wide World Photos; p. 45 © Lenny Ignelzi/AP/Wide World Photos; p. 47 © Yoshikazu Tsuno/AFP/Getty Images; p. 49 © Koji Sasahara/AP/Wide World Photos; p. 51 www.amazon.com; p. 52 www.news.google.com; p. 53 www.anonymizer.com.

Editor: Joann Jovinelly; Series Designer: Evelyn Horovicz
Photo Researcher: Hillary Arnold